Angelina Ballerina
and the
Tea Party

Based on the stories by Katharine Holabird
Based on the illustrations by Helen Craig

Ready-to-Read

Simon Spotlight
New York London Toronto Sydney New Delhi

SIMON SPOTLIGHT

An imprint of Simon & Schuster Children's Publishing Division

1230 Avenue of the Americas, New York, New York 10020

This Simon Spotlight edition December 2019

Illustrations by Mike Deas

For information about special discounts for bulk purchases, please contact Simon & Schuster Special Sales at

1-866-506-1949 or business@simonandschuster.com.

Manufactured in the United States of America 1019 LAK

10 9 8 7 6 5 4 3 2 1

ISBN 978-1-5344-5427-9 (hc)

ISBN 978-1-5344-5426-2 (pbk)

ISBN 978-1-5344-5428-6 (eBook)

On a sunny day
in Chipping Cheddar,
Angelina was planning
a tea party.

She invited
all her friends.

She chose
fancy teacups
and dishes.

Her friend Alice
came by to help.

They decorated
the table together.

"I would like to make
a fruit tart
for Miss Lilly,"
Angelina said.

"Can I have a taste?"
Alice giggled.

Then it was time
to get dressed.

Angelina and Alice had fun
choosing dresses
and hair ribbons.

Soon the guests
started to arrive.

"Hello, Henry,"
Angelina said.
"Have a seat!"

There were games,
music, and treats.

Everyone was having
a wonderful time.

Then Miss Lilly arrived.
"What a lovely tea party,"
she said.

"I have a surprise
for you,"
Angelina said.

She ran to the kitchen
to get the tart.

She was in such a hurry
that she tripped.
The tart fell on the floor!

"Oh no!"
Angelina cried.

Now she had nothing
to give Miss Lilly.

Then Angelina had an idea.
She could put on
a special dance
for Miss Lilly!

"I dropped the tart
I made for you,"
Angelina said sadly.

Then she began
to dance.

She jumped and twirled
toward Miss Lilly.

As she twirled
Angelina picked up
the teapot.
Then she poured tea
for Miss Lilly!

"Wow!" Henry said.
Angelina bowed,
and everyone clapped.

"Thank you,"
said Miss Lilly.
"I loved your dance."

"I have a surprise too,"
said Mrs. Mouseling.
"Cookies!"

"This is the best
tea party ever!"
Angelina cheered.